Izzy's Crossing

Written by
Donna M. Zappala

Illustrated by
Marco Serido

Children's Picture Book
Published on the Kittycat Books
label of Dragonfly Publishing, Inc.

THE air was fresh and warm.
  Spring had arrived.
  Izzy left her home in the salty marsh,
in search of higher ground.

"It's time to lay my eggs on the sandy beach," Izzy said, "but I don't know the way. Oh, I know! I'll ask someone."

Izzy saw a flock of herons greeting each other among the tall cord grass.

"Do you know the way to the sandy beach?" asked Izzy.

"Sorry," said the largest heron, "but we're in a hurry."

"Good luck with your travels," chorused the rest of the herons, as they took off in flight.

As Izzy waved goodbye to the herons, she noticed a snail shell near the blades of the coast.

Quickly, Izzy ate the snail. She had been in such a hurry to reach the sandy beach that she had forgotten to eat breakfast. The snail made a good meal.

With her stomach full, Izzy looked around for someone to show her the way to the sandy beach.

Then she noticed a toad sleeping behind a rock.

"Perhaps the toad knows the way," Izzy said.

"I'm sorry to disturb you," Izzy whispered to the toad, "but do you know the way to the sandy beach?"

"Don't bother me," said the grouchy toad as he rolled over. "I'm awake at night, but now is my sleepy time!"

"I'm tired, too," Izzy said with a yawn. "After a quick nap, I'll continue my search."

After a long slumber, Izzy awoke to find two big eyes staring into hers.

"I didn't mean to scare you, little terrapin," said a red fiddler crab.

"That's okay," Izzy replied. "I needed to wake up anyway. I'm trying to find the shore, so I can lay my eggs in the sand dunes. Do you know the way to the sandy beach?"

"I don't know the way," said the fiddler crab, "but I think I know someone who does. Follow me."

Izzy trailed behind the crab.

Unexpectedly, Izzy was back at the brackish marshland where her journey had begun.

There she saw a diamondback terrapin emerging from the water, just as she had done earlier that day.

"Izzy," said the fiddler crab, "I want you to meet Addie."

"It's nice to meet you," Addie said.

"It's nice to meet you, too," replied Izzy.

"Addie, I'm ready to lay my eggs," Izzy said. "Do you know the way to the sandy beach?"

"I do," Addie replied. "Would you like me to show you?"

"Yes, please," said Izzy.

"I hope you find your way, Izzy," said the fiddler crab.

Izzy kissed him on the cheek to show appreciation for all he had done for her.

Izzy and Addie began walking.
Soon the two terrapins came around a clump of dirt and stopped at the edge of a long, busy, noisy coastal road.

"Humans built this road
so they can easily reach the shore," Addie said.
    Izzy had never seen a human road. "Is
there another way to the beach?" she asked.
    With a sad expression, Addie shook her
head no.

Izzy had an idea how she and Addie could safely cross the road.

"I know," Izzy said. "We'll yell, sing, and dance about. Hopefully, the drivers will hear us and stop to let us cross."

"Let's give it a try," replied Addie.

At first no one heard Izzy and Addie.
Then a man pulled his car over to the side
of the road and leaned out his window. "Do
you need help?" he asked.

"We need to cross the road to reach the
sandy beach," explained Addie. "But the
cars will not stop for us."

After looking both ways, the man walked to the middle of the road and raised his hand to stop the traffic.

The cars stopped, allowing Izzy and Addie to cross the road safely.

As the terrapins crossed the road, they looked back at the man. "Thank you," they said together.

"With lots of kindness and support from my new friends, I finally found the way to the sandy beach," said Izzy. "Now it's time to lay my eggs."

She dug a nest and laid her eggs above high tide.

That summer, eight hatchling diamondback terrapins were born.

The End

Dedicated to all and my A, G and I in particular. Sometimes it takes a while to find your way. Don't give up because you never know when you might reach it. ~ Donna M. Zappala

IZZY'S CROSSING
Children's Picture Book [Rated G]

Paperback Edition
EAN 978-1-936381-61-6 | ISBN 1-936381-61-3

Story Text ©2014 Donna M. Zappala
Story Illustrations ©2014 Marco Serido
Dragonfly Logo ©2001 Terri L. Branson
Kittycat Books Logo ©2004 Terri L. Branson

Published in the United States of America by
Dragonfly Publishing, Inc. * www.dragonflypubs.com

Made in the USA
Charleston, SC
27 March 2014